Anonymous

Three Letters to the Right Hon. Edmund Burke

on the state of public affairs, and particularly on the late outrageous

attacks on his pension

Anonymous

Three Letters to the Right Hon. Edmund Burke
on the state of public affairs, and particularly on the late outrageous attacks on his pension

ISBN/EAN: 9783337734497

Printed in Europe, USA, Canada, Australia, Japan

Cover: Foto ©Andreas Hilbeck / pixelio.de

More available books at **www.hansebooks.com**

THREE
LETTERS

TO THE

Right Hon. Edmund Burke,

ON THE STATE OF

PUBLIC AFFAIRS;

AND

PARTICULARLY ON THE LATE

OUTRAGEOUS ATTACKS

ON HIS

PENSION.

***

BY AN OLD WHIG.

***

London:

PRINTED FOR G. G. AND J. ROBINSON, PATER-
NOSTER-ROW.

1796.

LETTER I.

TO THE RIGHT HONOURABLE.
EDMUND BURKE.

Sir,

THOUGH my admiration of your talents may be greatly difproportioned to your expectations, and to that adulation which you have been accuftomed to receive from your immediate flatterers and dependants, yet it would be unjuft to deny that I have generally derived pleafure from the perufal of your writings. They are the productions of a fertile and lively imagination, and of a mind not deftitute of energy; a mind which is ftored with learning, of a peculiar kind, with little indeed of fcientific, or ufeful knowledge, but with much of that defcription, which adminifters moft copioufly to entertainment. If, however, I have been amufed with your fancy, I have never found much reafon to compliment your judgment. Both your writings and your conduct feem effentially deficient in this quality—You " fnatch a grace beyond the reach of art"—Prudence feems with you

a vulgar

invulnerable, you have publicly fet yourfelf up, as the target, on which young markfmen may try their fkill with impunity and advantage—And I am forry to add, the mark is fo broad, that it is impoffible but that fome of the arrows fhould ftrike, and perhaps leave their barb in the wound.

You have challenged, and I forefee there will be no lack of combatants—" The infect youth." in the vicinity of St. Giles's, are already on the wing; already they begin to hum and buz—Already the monofyllable moft grateful to your ears, " Slides in a verfe, and hitches in a rhyme" —Already it ftands " rubric on the wall"—Already the names of Burke and Thelwall form a friendly coalition in large letters, on the vacant fpaces of public edifices—Already the caricature fhops are clearing their windows for your reception—" The old man with a young penfion"--- " The two-faced orator, with one to the king, and another to the people," and a thoufand pretty devices of the fame nature, are even now, I underftand, in agitation.

Is it poffible, that this is a kind of fame, of which you are ambitious ? I recollect, indeed, that I have before difcovered in you, fymptoms of this difpofition.

difpofition. If, then, fame and notoriety are your objects, you will have them; but remember that if you have them, you muft pay the price, you muft take the evil with the good---Remember too, that whatever you may fuffer, you have brought it on yourfelf. You have really prefcribed and defined the laws of the conteft---If you fuffer from perfonal calumny, you have, by your example, invited retaliation; you have called for afperity of language, and a fevere examination of your public conduct. If, therefore, your fkin, like John Zifca's, according to your own elegant allufion, is to be converted into an inftrument of terror; remember that you have formed, and fitted, and carved the drumfticks yourfelf; and if by this, or any other medium, an alarm can be founded through the regions of corruption, it will certainly be more advantageous to mankind, than that harfh, difcordant *war-whoop*, which you vociferate with all the clamour of an uncivilized barbarian.

Your ambition indeed, Sir, of late has affumed a moft fingular and prepofterous character. There was a time when you would lefs have valued the praifes of Lord Grenville; there was a time when you treated the " School-boy" ftatefmen with lefs refpect; and when you at leaft affected to be lefs callous to the contempt of great

and

and independent characters. For my part, I do not hesitate to assert, that I would prefer a single sentence of commendation from such men, to the most laboured eulogy that the hard heads of . I Grenville, Sir Watkin Lewis, Sir John ..... Sir James Saunderson, Lord Abingdon, ... Alderman Curtis, could painfully produce. .... I have heard of a man whose taste and ear were so lamentably depraved, as to prefer the brayings of a jack-ass to the most enchanting strains of a Handel.

In making a few remarks on your Letter, I should wish, if it were possible, to preserve some lucid order, some regular plan ; but its texture is so unequal, its arrangement so diftorted, that I am at a loss where to begin, or what method to pursue. It is extremely difficult to conjecture what relation there can be between your pension and the French Revolution ; your 4000l. per annum, and the present hopeful war ; in your own mind there may be some whimsical association between these topics, for I observe that the mention of the one inevitably brings the other to your re-collection. It would have been candid in you to explain this connexion ; under which of the moral relations it is to be clasfed, whether under that of cause and effect, of contiguity, or resemblance, or

con-

contrariety. Had you done this, I might perhaps have been able to reply to your firſt four pages, which at preſent, for want of this explanation, appear neither more nor leſs than rhapſody.

To elude the difficulty you tell us that common minds, that is men of plain common ſenſe, and men verſed in arithmetic, geometry, and ſuch vulgar ſciences, " cannot readily comprehend the tranſaction," and in this I perfectly agree with you—We really do not *comprehend* the nature of the tranſaction in queſtion; yet, I am much miſtaken, if it is not in your power to explain it.

" It was the fruit of no bargain ; the production of no intrigue ; the reſult of no compromiſe ; the effect of no ſolicitation."—Now, Sir, is it poſſible that you can be ſo weak, as to flatter yourſelf for a moment, that there exiſts in this country a ſingle man ſo ſtupidly credulous as to be blinded by theſe aſſertions ? Is the miniſter that frank and liberal friend of genius, that he forces, and heaps his favours on the deſerving ; with no view, no intereſt, no intrigue ? Let the moral merits of Mr. Dundas and Mr. Roſe ; let the brilliant talents of Sir John Mitford, of Mr. Brooke Watſon, of Mr. Alderman Le Meſurier, and Mr. Alderman Curtis, and a long train of worthies in

church

church and state, vouch for this assertion. The late loan was undoubtedly a simple effort to reward genius and virtue. The war itself was entered into merely to call merit out of obscurity; and the office of *third secretary of state* was revived, contrary to both the letter and the spirit of your own Bill, only to give a scope to the profound penetration, the splendid abilities, and the deep political wisdom, of that great statesman the Duke of Portland.

How disinterested towards his own family and connexions!—How negligent of himself is this Heaven-born minister! How indifferent to election jobs; to the gaining of suffrages both in and out of the house! What a patron of literature has he ever shewn himself—and after this you will say: " Can any man doubt that my pension has been obtained by the most honourable means? No connexions to be gained—No dupes to be made—No pamphlets to be written—No man's character and ancestry to be libelled"---No, No!!!

Yet there is something mysterious in the transaction after all. If your pension be really the reward of your past services; of your reform in the pay-office; of your reform in the civil list; why did not the minister embrace the first opportunity of
rewarding

rewarding you after his acceſſion to office ? Why was the meed of virtue delayed till a period of life, when, according to your own ſtatement, it can ſcarcely be of advantage to you ? " Had you died," as you obſerve in this long interim, you "had earn-ed" your penſion ; but you would not have had it ; and, alas ! I can eaſily ſee that " thoſe who be-longed to you" would not have had it.—Is this then the way that liberality and public ſpirit diſ-penſe public and liberal rewards ? For ten long years and more, the prudent Chancellor has cho-ſen to pauſe, before he could determine whether you had merited his bounty or not.—Would to Heaven he had been equally cautious, ſlow, and circumſpeℭt in all his meaſures ! We ſhould not now have to bewail his raſhneſs in tears of blood ; to curſe from the bottom of our hearts his boyiſh ambition.

Sir, it was at a very ſuſpicious period, indeed, that the miniſter's heart and hand were opened.—It was at a period, when two mad ſchemes had been defeated by the union and energy of the Whig Party ; and juſt when another hopeful projeℭt had taken poſſeſſion of his brain. Then was it neceſ-ſary to thin the ranks, and deſtroy the aℭtivity of this formidable phalanx. To throw among you the golden apple of diſcord, and, by their eager-

C   neſs

neſs to catch it, to render ſome of you for ever contemptible.

When you modeſtly inform us that your merits are incomprehenſible, I feel diſpoſed to agree with you. When you ſet vulgar arithmetic at defiance, and hold it in conrempt, I am leſs inclined to aſſent. Vulgar arithmetic I cannot but hold to be a uſeful ſcience, though the reſult of its calculations may be a little aukward on ſome occaſions— I dare predict, for inſtance, that the miniſter would be glad that Mr. Sheridan and Mr. Morgan * underſtood this vulgar ſcience no better than himſelf. Yet, on the other hand, the nation has cauſe to wiſh that their Chancellor of the Exchequer would pay a little attention to ſuch inveſtigations. If he did, we ſhould not now have to lament an accumulation of one hundred and forty millions to the public debt from his diſaſtrous adminiſtration.— We ſhould not, perhaps, be preſſed down with taxes; our reſources daily diminiſhing; while one inauſpicious loan is improvidently raiſed to make good deficiencies, and pay the intereſt of another.

* See a pamphlet which every Engliſhman ought to read, entitled, " Facts, addreſſed to the ſerious Attention of the People of Great Britain."

When

When you speak of " the theory of moral proportions," and " of the rule of three, in the arithmetic of policy and state," indeed, Sir, I am obliged to plead the same incorrigible ignorance
with which you stigmatise the Duke of Bedford.
I am a plain man, and the arithmetic of metaphysics I do not understand ; and what is more, I have
never yet been fortunate enough to meet with a
man that was able to explain it to me. I cannot
help it, Sir, but I am inclined to suspect, that this
is neither more nor less than what we term *jargon*;
and an old man with new nonsense, is just as ridiculous as a young man with *old* absurdities. Whatever is incomprehensible to plain and undepraved
reason is *jargon*; and I have often thought it difficult to decide, which party excells most in that
figure of speech, which is called the unintelligible,
Mr. Burke, or the new philosophers.

When, however, you come to speak of services,
you then seem to descend from the high and cloudy
regions of metaphysics, and come within the scope
of a common man's capacity. But I will not
depreciate your services, by supposing that the
enumeration of them can be consistent with the
limits of this letter. I shall, therefore, from pure
respect, dedicate my next epistle entirely to their
consideration. But it is something extraordinary,

C 2   that

that thefe fervices have never been till lately difcovered ; it is fomething not lefs extraordinary,
that you are obliged to tell us of them yourfelf. It
is very extraordinary, that fo difcerning a perfon
as the Marquis of Rockingham, fhould not have
feen them in their proper light, and that the rewarding of them fhould have been left to the
adminiftration of Mr. Pitt.

"Penfion for myfelf," you fay (alluding I prefume
to the Rockingham adminiftration), " I obtained
none."—Which, by the way, reminds me a little
of a certain inflated tranflation of Tacitus—" At
this time war there was none." A tale, however,
has been told (and this tale unfortunately remains
uncontradicted) of a certain great orator, who
obtained a penfion on the Irifh eftablifhment of
1500l. per annum. This penfion he chofe to have
in *another* name, becaufe, I prefume, he was *then*
afhamed of appearing as a ftipendiary. Whether
this penfion or annuity was mortgaged, or fold,
or in what manner it was difpofed of, is little to
our prefent purpofe. If it was, it would only
ferve to prove your pofition, that the houfe of
Ruffel underftand vulgar arithmetic better than
certain great metaphyfical philofophers — They
have kept their property undiminifhed through
revolving ages ; this great orator has been obliged,
through

through improvidence, to fell one penfion, and bargain for another.

With thefe few obfervations I fhall wifh you a good night; to-morrow I fhall prefent you with a few more in the fame plain ftyle—

———————— " Read this,
" And this, and this, and then to breakfaft
With what appetite you may."

I am, Sir, your's, &c.

Weftpark, March 3,
1796.

R. P.

LETTER II.

Sir,

THERE are no publications which contribute more to general entertainment; I might add, to general information and improvement, than thofe in which the author lays open the receffes of his own heart, the fecret hiftory of his motives, his intentions and his conduct. I do not approve of the prudence of the authors, but the utility of fuch productions I am always willing to admit. It is not always neceffary that thefe narratives fhould contain nothing but pictures of wifdom and of virtue. Whatever they may be, they fhew us human nature, and human life. I can, therefore, perufe, with pleafure, the Confeffions of Roufeau, and of Mr. Burke; the Life of Major Semple, and the no lefs interefting adventures of any political fwindler.

I have expected latterly, with fome impatience, a detail of the motives which induced you to embark in projects of reform, and I am happy, in your prefent work (which may be ftyled your Confeffions)

I

feffions) to find at leaft an *ingenicus* explanation of what appeared fo inconfiftent with the political doctrines which you have lately publifhed as the governing maxims of your conduct.

In ftating your fervices, you have been, as ufual, rather prolix *. You have contrived to envelope a *very little* folid fterling matter in a huge matrix of a certain bafe and ufelefs production, which the French call *verbiage*. I can, however, eafily forgive " the importance of a man to himfelf," nor is it the firft time you have evinced, that you have ftudied with effect the " Memoirs of P. P. clerk " of this parifh." After fome difficulty in developing the facts from the mafs of words, in which they are involved, it appears that you confine your claims to merit, to three principal objects : the reform in the pay-office; the reform in the civil lift; and the India affairs, alias, the profecution of Mr. Haftings.

---

* Mr. Burke, from his long fpeeches, was called the dinner bell of the Houfe of Commons, as when he rofe to fpeak, it had generally the effect of clearing the houfe. His antipapathy, indeed, in the firft inftance, to the French revolution, is attributed to a witticifm common in the national affembly as it was ufual when a member was proceeding in a tedious and uninterefting fpeech, to cry out—" Point à la Burke !" ·

Where

Where very grofs and flagrant abufes exift, they exift not becaufe they are undifcovered and unknown, but becaufe they are connived at for particular ends, and corrupt purpofes. The difficulty is not to find out a remedy, but to obtain fufficient influence to apply that remedy. Thus, as to the abufes in the pay-office, they were known to thoufands; and you made a clamour (while in oppofition) concerning thefe abufes, and you committed yourfelf too far to retract. When you came in with the Rockingham adminiftration, you acted with honourable men, who, for the fake of their own character, could not have permitted this Augean ftable to remain totally uncleanfed, after what you had advanced upon the fubject, had you been ever fo willing. But, if I am not miftaken, there is not a clerk in that office, who would not, if properly fupported, have been able to effect a much more complete reform, than you effected, with half the clamour, and who would not have thought himfelf amply compenfated for the whole labour by one half the amount of one year's income from your penfion.

In enumerating your fervices in this office, your modefty, however, has led you to omit one, which ftands prominent above the reft, in the eyes of every man of fenfe and probity. You have omitted

to

to ftate, that you have replaced in offices of truft in that department two men who had been difmiffed for fraud, peculation, and public robbery; who were at that moment under a criminal profecution for their offences. You endeavoured to fcreen them from juftice by your influence and eloquence. One of them had rather more modefty and con- fcience than his unblufhing patron and defender, and removed himfelf, by an act (which God forbid I fhould juftify) from public difgrace; and with refpect to the other, a common jury, who judged by the rules of vulgar arithmetic, and not by the new fcale of moral proportions, rectified your de- cifion.

If I underftand rightly your account of your other projects of reform, they amount to what is termed in plain and *vulgar* language, a *humbug.* The people wanted a reality, and you put them off with a fhadow; they called for reform, and you determined to give them fomething elfe, which might pleafe and gratify them.---A noftrum of your own preparing, which I grant the *exifling cir- cumftances* of the nation, and the very fubject of your prefent appeal, prove was of very little effi- cacy in reftricting the influence of the crown. It was fomething which was to act like animal mag- netifm, not on the *body* politic, but on the imagi-

D   nation

nation of the patient. You, however, did not be-
have with the accuftomed generofity of your bre-
thren in Moorfields, who, with at leaft the *femblance*
of *honefty*, place in large letters on their bills, the
alluring fentence,---" No cure no pay."—
—You require an enormous reward for doing—nothing; and you now pleafantly tell us, that though
you effected nothing to the purpofe, yet you perhaps prevented your patient from falling into the
hands of fome more defperate and ignorant quack
than yourfelf. I was, at that time, a much younger
man than I am now, and I remember I thought
Lord Thurlow illiberal for the obfervations which
he made upon your plans, which he termed " A
" puny regulation, only calculated to deceive and
" betray the people."—You have now burft the
bubble yourfelf, and come forward with fome fhare
of modeft affurance, to boaft how handfomely you
duped us; and folemnly to affure us " that it was
" not your love but your hatred to innovation, that
" produced the plan of reform."

In the fame happy ftyle you inform us concerning the fund out of which your penfion is granted :
" This of the 4½ per cents. does his grace imagine
" had efcaped me ?" The event fhows that it did
not efcape you; and moft men will *now* give you
credit for what you affirm, that the *fund* from
which

which a penfion might iffue was always " full in " your eye." But I afk you, Sir, not what you thought, but what you profeffed? for, by your own account of yourfelf, we are never to look upon your intentions, but upon your profeffions. I afk you then ferioufly to anfwer me, if you can anfwer a plain queftion in plain words.

Did you not know that this fund was folemnly appropriated by the authority of the legiflature by which it was raifed, for the defence *only* of the Leeward iflands; as appears in the act paffed by the affembly of Barbadoes in 1663?

Have you never declared, when you were afked why this fund was not included in your reform bill, that the reafon was, that this fund was otherwife appropriated, and no penfion could be legally granted upon it?

Did you not applaud Lord Thurlow's conduct, when he refufed to put the feal to the penfion which was to have been granted to Lord Aukland, iffuing out of this fund, upon the grounds that every fuch grant was illegal?

Though you have been thus induftrious to exhibit yourfelf to the public in the character of a

C 2

bottle

bottle conjurer—as the Katterfelto of the Houfe of, Commons, I, Sir, am more willing to do you juftice, than you are yourfelf. I believe you were, at one period at leaft, in earneft in your projects of reform, becaufe it fuited your purpofe, and becaufe you acted in concert with honourable and honeft men, the Rockinghams and the Savilles. You muft remember that you lamented in the ftrongeft terms, that you were *not able* to effect more in the caufe of reform. You now take advantage of this circumftance, and make a merit of your impotence. You know the *ftuff* (to fpeak in your own language) of which the men with whom you now act, are made ; you know they are fhallow, though cunning. *They*, I believe, are the dupes, and not the public. Becaufe you are not *able*, you perfuade them that you were not *willing* to do more. If, therefore, you can make them believe that you were *falfe* and infincere in your former profeffions, I dare fay it will enhance your merit with them. That you are *now* an apoftate is certainly no mean recommendation; if you can perfuade them that you were *always* a *hypocrite*, it will doubtlefs double, at leaft, your value in the eyes of Mr. Pitt and Lord Grenville, who feem to adopt, pretty much the fame rules of " moral " proportion" with yourfelf.

This

This obfervation may poffibly lead to an explanation of that fingular *equivoque*, or mental refervation, which I know has embarraffed fome fenfible perfons, who have read your Pamphlet---You " hold one language to your opponents, and another to the King." To the one you boaft of your fervices; ---" before the prefence of the other you claim no merit at all; every thing there is favour, is bounty." Indeed, Sir, it would not be an eafy tafk to prove what the fervices are which you have rendered to the King. No man, in my opinion, can have lefs occafion to thank you for your paft fervices than the King---He cannot thank you in his heart. I will affirm that no man's writings and fpeeches were ever more calculated to bring Kings into contempt than your's : no not thofe of Thomas Paine himfelf. Revife them, Sir, even in the garbled edition to which you refer, if you doubt my affertion. Perhaps in the eye of " a mild and benevolent Sovereign," you may derive fome merit from repentance---I am glad you have repented---I venerate the conftitution and the monarchy---I fcorn equally the metaphyfical doctrines of Paine and of Burke ; I have often (and on one occafion in particular) felt indignant at the indecency of your expreflions when fpeaking of the Majefty of England. But forgivenefs and reward are extremely different. That, as a penitent,

you

you deferved to be forgiven, I admit; but that, as a penitent, you fhould claim a reward of 4000l. per annum, is an infult on common fenfe.

On the fubject of the affairs of India, I muft fay, it would have become you to be filent. The leaft conceffion that can be expected from the *falfe accufer* is, that in obfcurity and modeft filence he fhould hide his diminifhed head---But it is a fafhion with the *new* philofophers, or *new* ftatefmen fhall I call them? (for every thing now is new) to arraign the moft folemn adjudications of the moft folemn tribunals. Your difciple Mr. Wyndham has difcovered that men who have been declared " not guilty," by the verdict and voice of their country, are " only acquitted felons;" and you, after Mr. Haftings has been abfolved by the higheft court of judicature eftablifhed by this conftitution, obftinately and perverfely claim a degree of merit for having inftituted a vexatious fuit, for having caufed the nation fruitlefsly to expend more than even the value of your penfion, for having created quarrels, raifed ill-founded fufpicions, and exhibited a mighty farce, which, in my opinion, was far from honourable to either the Lords or the Commons of Great Britain.

Our *liberal* adminiftration, however, who concurred

curred with you in urging the profecution, have feen their error, and have, I underftand, voted Mr. Haftings a compenfation for his fufferings.— Let it be recorded among the ever memorable curiofities of the eighteenth century, among the wonders of a wonder-working minifter---" Mr. Burke was penfioned for profecuting Mr. Haftings; and Mr. Haftings for having been profecuted !"

Did you difplay your knowledge of India affairs by the palpable falfehoods which you afferted in your opening fpeech ?---Did you difplay your fpirit in maintaining your affertions, when Captain Williams called you to account ?

Of your fervices to Ireland I will candidly confefs my inability to decide. I want documents and proof to enable me to fpeak pofitively either to the affirmative or the negative of the queftion---You fay, " My endeavour was to obtain liberty for the municipal country in which I was born, and for all defcriptions and denominations in it"---If I may fpeak my fentiments freely, and I fpeak them fubject to your correction, it is my opinion, that whatever Ireland has obtained, was obtained, not by your endeavours, but by her own energy, fenfe, and fpirit. Your endeavours, I fufpect, were confined to your *good wifhes*, and even thofe wifhes

were reftricted to a particular defcription of men---
Yet I rejoice in the emancipation of Ireland (as far
as it has been effected) from civil and religious op-
preffion; and if you have had any fhare in thefe reforms, as foon as you can *prove* your merits, I will
give you full credit for them, whatever might be
the religious prejudices under which you acted.
The laws againft the Catholics in Ireland were a
fyftem of robbery, a ftanding libel on every principle of juftice. Like fome of the cruel regula-
tions of Sparta, they feemed, as if they had been
enacted to encourage chicanery, and to hold out a
public recompence for fraud. I have heard narratives of their effects, difgufting to every natural
feeling and fympathy of man---Narratives (*fabulous*
perhaps) but the bare poffibility of which is fhock-
ing to humanity, and difgraceful to legiflation. I
have heard of trufts executed under the moft facred
oaths and engagements, which have been converted, by the perverfion of law, into inftruments
to defraud the orphan and the widow. I have
heard of eftates committed in confidence and
friendfhip to the tutelage of others; and I have
heard of their being wrefted from their lawful pof-
feffors by the operation of thefe odious ftatutes;
and even vefting in the families of thofe who committed the firft violation of a facred truft. I fhould
hope that thefe random reports are only the *fictions*

of

of Catholics, to fhew in more glaring colours the legal flavery under which they were reduced; but ftill they were *poffible*, while the ftatutes in queftion exifted, and though I am no admirer of the Popifh fuperftitions, yet I fincerely, for the fake of juftice, rejoice with you, that thefe oppreffive ftatutes exift no more.

If you can prove that you have been inftrumental in obtaining redrefs for this injured clafs of men, I fhall be the firft to acknowledge your merits; but for your other fervices, which you affirm *money could not reward*, I cannot affent to your poftulate, that " they are more than the Duke of Bedford's ideas of fervice are of power to eftimate?" ---I can only agree in your conclufion, that you ought not to have had your *reward in money*; your reward ought to have been of a very different nature.---I believe, Sir, I can draw up a much more correct bill of cofts and charges for you than you have drawn up for yourfelf; and in fpite of your averfion to vulgar arithmetic, I fhall adopt the ufual forms, as it will anfwer the purpofe of perfpicuity, at leaft to vulgar readers, better than your fyftem of " moral proportions"---

E   The

The Britifh Nation Debtor,

        To the Right Hon. Edmund Burke.

	£	s.	d.
For my great and meritorious fervices in his Majefty's kitchen	0	0	0
For obliging the King and Queen, of an opulent nation, to eat by contract, like the inhabitants of a workhoufe	0	0	0
For weeping over the tattered fhirt and breeches of the Jew, worfted in a certain fcuffle at St. Euftatia	0	0	0
For defending Powell and Bembridge - -	0	0	0
For the fublime difcovery, that " Kings are always lovers of low company" - -	0	0	0
For " hurling the King from his throne" - -	0	0	0
For the facetious and elegant ftories of Deby Sing, prince Cantemir, &c. &c. told for the entertainment of the ladies of the court	0	0	0
For deferting and abufing all my old friends and connexions	26,000	0	0

For humanely endeavouring to provoke all Europe to maffacre

                                    each

	£.	s.	d.
each other, and to embroil England in an unneceſſary quarrel, which has already coſt the nation only 140 millions -	9,999	19	$9\frac{1}{2}$
For the celebrated dagger ſcene in the Houſe of Commons -	0	0	$2\frac{1}{2}$
Total amount of my penſion for ſix lives, at nine years purchaſe -	36,000	0	0

The above account I have ſuppoſed to be checked, as in the courſe of buſineſs, by the Chancellor of his Majeſty's Exchequer—But any of the items ſhall be rectified on a proper application from yourſelf, as I really do not wiſh to wrong or miſrepreſent you.

I am, Sir, your's, &c.

Weſtpark, March 4,
1796.

R. P.

LET-

LETTER III.

SIR,

IN my former Letter, I had occaſion to notice the obligations which you have conferred upon the King, and the ſervices which you have rendered to the cauſe' of monarchy; but I really did not know, till I read your laſt publication, the extent of thoſe favours which you have conferred on the ancient ariſtocracy of the realm; I did not know that you had determined to act with ſuch an impartial hand; to diſtribute juſtice with ſo nice and even a ballance, that you would leave no room for complaint on the part of the nobility, of the partiality which you had previouſly demonſtrated to kings.

This is a ſubject, Sir, which I ſhall have preſently to notice, and you may depend upon it the Republicans will notice it too. Your ſhaft is at preſent avowedly directed at the Duke of Bedford; and becauſe he was born to high rank and great fortune, it is your object to perſuade your readers, that he is deſtitute of talents. I am not, Sir, the official defender of his grace, I have only under-
taken

taken to unmaſk *you*; and to ſhew you that I know
you better than you ſeem to ſuſpect it poſſible for
any man to know you *, I will tell you, that it is
not his grace's rank or fortune that has terrified
you on this occaſion ;—it is his talents. This cir-
cumſtance it is that has rendered you captious,
querulous, and vindictive. Had he not been poſ-
ſeſſed of talents, let his fortune be what it would,
like ſome other dukes and peers, with whom both
you and I can boaſt a ſlight acquaintance, he might
quietly have dozed upon the benches of the Houſe
of Lords, without any penſioned libeller attempt-
ing to diſturb his repoſe.

Leſt we ſhould, however, miſtake your real aim
and object, you tell us that your introduction of
the Duke of Bedford on the ſtage, is to ſerve as a
mere *vehicle*, " to convey your ſentiments on matters far more worthy of attention"---The abſtract
ſubject immediately connected with this ſentence is
hereditary nobility---and the inference is, that you
deſire your remarks to be abſtractly applied. I
have indeed always ſuſpected, that Thomas Paine
(with whom I underſtand you were once intimate)
and you have more opinions in common than you

* Naturaliſts tell us of a certain animal, which, when it
conceals its head, ſuppoſes that becauſe it ſees nobody, it is
impoſſible any perſon ſhould ſee it.

have

have avowed. This at leaſt I am ſure of, that neither he nor Joel Barlow has treated the privi- leged orders with more diſreſpect than you have, in the very publication that lies before me. The only difference between you is this, that they have written in the abſtract, as upon a ſpeculative ſub- ject ; you have choſen to perſonify---They have laid down general principles ; you have deſcended to particulars---They have argued upon hypothe- ſis and conjecture ; you have inſtanced---They ſaid exactly the ſame things that you have ſaid ; but I will grant they have not ſaid them ſo well.

To be a member of the Houſe of Peers, ac- cording to your *new* politico-philoſophy, is to be " Swaddled, and rocked, and dandled into a legi- ſlator ;" I recollect a paſſage exactly ſimilar in one of theſe writers, but not half ſo forcibly expreſſed. The nobility, you inſinuate, " have an hereditary privilege to be fools ;" " The arts that recommend men to the favour and protection of the great," are to be " a minion or a tool"---" To follow the trade of winning hearts, by impoſing on the under- ſtandings of the people." In expoſing the origin of nobility, and the enormity and profligacy of " grants from the crown," how ſucceſsful would republican critics eſteem you ? Their effect is to create " Leviathans" in the ſtate---The royal " lion

" lion firft fucks the blood of his prey, and throws
the offal to the jackal in waiting." The merits of
the nobility are not " original and perfonal, but
derivative;" nay, if one of a race happens not to
be a " minion," and " an inftrument," he " de-
generates into virtue"---" The herald's college,
however, " feek no further merit than the pream-
ble to a patent, or the infcription on a tomb; they
judge of every man's capacity by the offices he has
filled"---Are we reading citizen Paine, or citizen
Barlow, or the abbé Sieyes?---No, gentle reader,
it is no other than Mr. Burke!

I pafs over your notorious breach of the privileges of the houfe. I venerate thefe privileges
upon principle. You may call this principle
a prejudice, perhaps, when it fuits you to difpenfe
with it, though no man was more ready to enforce
it, when you were perfonally concerned. Even
prejudices, Sir, are in fome meafure refpectable,
when united with confiftency. But even principles
lofe reverence in the eyes of the multitude, when
thofe who moft ftrongly contend for them, are the
firft to violate them for private ends or felfifh purpofes.

It has, indeed, been faid of you, with fome
fhrewdnefs, that " you have turned king's evidence
againft

against the aristocracy"---and I have quoted your
sentiments, I assure you, not as approving them.
It is certain that rank neither confers talents, nor
precludes them—Hereditary nobles are like other
men, with respect to capacity.   They possess some
advantages of education, and I believe the proportion of men of parts among them, is much the
same as among other men, who have had similar
advantages.   Some, like the Duke of Bedford and
the Earl of Lauderdale, reflect a lustre by their
talents, their spirit, and their independence, on
the conspicuous stations in which they are placed ;
some serve as the mere passive ornaments of a
court, which they decorate on a birth-day, or some
similar solemnity.   In their collective capacity,
they are placed as a barrier between the usurpations
of prerogative, and the clamours of democracy.
Our history abounds in instances where they have
successfully withstood both.   To the aristocracy of
England we are indebted for no small portion of
our liberties—For the Magna Charta---For the re-
formation, by the protection which some of them afforded, in its early stages, to the persecuted reformers,
and by the spirit with which they resisted the papal
usurpations---For the glorious Revolution, which the
aristocracy planned and effected.   The aristocracy re-
lieved the nation from the calamities and horrors of
the American war—and if the national spirit is now
sunk

funk and degraded, it is to be attributed to the corrupt and overwhelming influence of a pernicious monied aristocracy; to a new created, mushroom aristocracy, and not to the ancient nobility of the realm.

Your pedigree of the Duke of Bedford I do not mean at present to dispute. I would only observe, that your statement, relative to the fate of the Duke of Buckingham, &c. is directly contrary to the testimony of Hume and other respectable historians; and I suspect that you have only been guilty of a mistake of about twenty years, which, with you, is to be sure a trifling anachronism; for I believe " the first peer of the house of Ruffel" did not come into office, notice, or power, till about twenty years after the decease of the Duke of Buckingham; and if he had been at that period in office, he could be no further concerned in that or any other of the transactions you would impute to him, than the rest of the privy-council, who were a numerous body. He was no prime minister, though I grant that he was raised from the station of a respectable private gentleman, and was ennobled and enriched by the favour of his Sovereign. But supposing every word you have afferted to be fact, how illiberal is the charge, when applied to a descendant of the family, after a lapse of two

F   hundred

hundred years! You would deem it unworthy conduct in any man who was to upbraid you with being the fon of an obfcure pettifogging attorney in Dublin. Such a *circumftance* cannot affect your merits: and you certainly pay the Duke of Bedford a high compliment, when the heavieft crime you can lay to his charge, is, that one of his remote anceftors was a *Courtier*. But I perceive your object—You would deftroy the hereditary refpect, ingrafted in the hearts of Englifhmen for the houfe of Ruffel.—You fhall never eradicate it, while we venerate our conftitution and our liberties! That refpect can only be annihilated by the mifconduct of that houfe themfelves. In the prefent reprefentative of that honoured name, the fpirit of his anceftor (not him whom you have reviled, but one whom even you cannot revile) furvives.—He is, and muft be dear to the people.—If you wifh to degrade and difgrace the houfe of Ruffel, it will not be effected by impotent libels againft him; but by perfuading him, if you can, to imitate your conduct. It is not your enmity, Mr. Burke, that can deftroy popularity, it is your friendfhip.

You have affigned an origin and pedigree to the Duke of Bedford, which would, perhaps, better fuit many of the moft opulent and refpectable families in this kingdom—But have you confidered

the

the ruinous confequences of this levelling principle?—Do you not perceive that it extends not
merely to the annihilation of nobility, but of property itfelf? If no man have a lawful claim to
property, but he whofe anceftors obtained it by
the faireft and moft honourable means, who among
us can be fafe in his poffeffions? This is worfe
than French Democracy; this is more than the
Convention itfelf, in the very madnefs of confifca-
tion, has dared to affume.

I hope I have read, with a proper portion of
fympathy and humanity, your affecting and elegant
tribute to the memory of your fon. Sorrow is
ever facred in my eyes—I will not enquire into
the truth and correctnefs of the eulogium, nor
difturb the afhes, you wifh to embalm. Let him
be all that you defcribe, and more, if it will eafe your
heart of a fingle pang—I pity you from my foul.—

I pity you more than ordinary men.—I pity you,
becaufe in your partiality to that fon, I fee the
only apology that can be offered for your paft conduct. It is a tribute which in juftice I owe to you,
to fay, that I believe you have been the dupe of
parental fondnefs. I believe, to that fon you facri-
ficed your reputation, your character, your prefent and your future peace. I believe, that to make

him

him great, you made yourself little. I believe that
it was to obtain a splendid and lucrative establish-
ment for that son, that, by a fatal desertion of party
and of principles, you at one blow demolished the
fair fabric of fame, which you had been erecting,
and became the abject tool of a minister, whose
talents you ever held in just contempt; whose
puerile arrogance must even now disgust you; and
whose little and contemptible arts must be offen-
sive to a mind of any dignity, of any cultivation.

To pass from a subject which cannot be grateful
to you (the comparison of what you were, with
what you are) to one which is more within my
province, and my object; I cannot admit the
justice of the analogy, which you endeavour to
establish between your pension, and an ancient grant
from the crown. A grant of lands from the crown,
at the period in question, stands upon a footing
entirely different from your's. At that period,
happily for the nation, there was no public debt
to be redeemed. Lands fell to the crown, by the
ordinary process of law.—Whether the sentence by
which they escheated was just or unjust, is a question foreign to the purpose. These lands must
have a possessor, and the king assigned them, according to his prerogative, to that possessor whom
he esteemed most deserving of them. If the King,
after

after they came into his poffeffion, impoverifhed any perfon, it was himfelf: and no friend of liberty would wifh that the crown had retained poffeffion of the immenfe eftates which were added to the royal demefnes by the legal courfe of efcheat and forfeiture. But your penfion, Sir, is wrung by heavy and cruel taxes, in times of public diftrefs, from an oppreffed and fuffering people. The half-famifhed cottager, who receives the miferable pittance of *fixteen-pence* a day for the fubfiftence of perhaps an infant family, pays a portion of that *fixteen-pence* to maintain you in luxury. You fay you " have not more than fufficient"—Believe me, I am truly forry for the affertion. If your penfion was meant for your future fubfiftence, it is certainly " more than fufficient" for the fupport of a man of letters and a philofopher: if it was meant for the fupply of former deficiencies *, the fact is not more to your credit. The man who, through extravagance or profufion, lofes his independence, lofes every fafeguard of virtue and of honour; he lays himfelf open to the approaches of the tempter;

---

* It is a remarkable circumftance, that of the two branches or annuities which compofe Mr. Burke's penfion, one (I believe the larger) is fecured upon three young lives, not one of whom is of his own family. The other is fecured upon two young lives, neither of them of his own family, with the infertion only of his own name in it, though not in the former.

he

he becomes neceffarily the tool, the fport of bad men for bad purpofes. I have heard, indeed, circumftances relative to the negociation for your penfion, with the repetition of which I fhall not wound you at prefent. I have heard of difficulties and embarraffments, and I was forry to hear them; Such were not the *old Whigs*—Such was not Andrew Marvel, whofe character you once, I am told, *profeffed yourfelf* ambitious to emulate.

Your tranfition is happy from the grants of the crown and your own penfion, to the French Revolution; but the conclufion you would deduce from it, is not quite fo logical, as the tranfition is ftriking. I will difrobe it of metaphor, and put your argument in the form of a fyllogifm, for you love fometimes the dialect of the fchools; and your education in St. Stephen's Chapel has not quite obliterated the rudiments you learned at St. Omer's.

The French Revolution originated in complaints of the lavifh Expenditure of the public money :
But the Duke of Bedford, and the Earl of Lauderdale have thought my penfion among the inftances of lavifh Expenditure :
Ergo, the Duke of Bedford, and the Earl of Lauderdale wifh to produce a Revolution in this country fimilar to that of France.

In

In this fyllogifm the *major* is indeed unquef-
tionable; but the confequence is illogical. It was
indeed by a profufion of penfions, falaries, grants,
loans, and contracts, that the French finances became irrecoverably deranged. The intereft of
the public debt could no longer be paid, and no
additional taxes could poffibly be levied. But a
timely and prudent infpection into the national expenditure; the abolition of finecure and unnecef-
fary places; the reduction of unmerited penfions;
and the difpofal of contracts, commiffions, and
loans, by fair and open competition, would have
prevented that moft calamitous cataftrophe, which
I lament perhaps more fincerely than you do.

The rights of man were never dreamt of in
France, till every right was invaded by the neceffities, or feeming neceffities of the ftate; till the
rapacity of courtiers, and the improvidence of a
fpendthrift adminiftration, who, like the prefent
minifters of this country, paid the intereft of one
loan by creating a new one, had left men nothing
they could call their own, and had virtually annihilated all property in the nation, except that which
was vefted in the hands of the privileged orders, or
in the hands of a few monied men, who were neceffary to the corruption and extravagance of the
court. This is the true fecret hiftory of the French
Revolution;

Revolution; and I sincerely hope and pray that
" the example of France may operate as a warn-
ing to Britain."

Is it then confistent with logic, with sense, with
honesty, to insinuate, that because the Duke of Bedford and the Earl of Lauderdale, and those patriots
who act with them, whose worth will be revered
by future generations as much as it is disregarded
by the present; because they would have prevented
by negociation the most ruinous, the most bloody,
and most expensive war in which this nation ever
was engaged, a war which the minister had neither
sense to avoid, nor abilities to conduct; because
they recommended a prudent œconomy in every
branch of administration; is it for these reasons
that you charge them with endeavouring to produce a revolution; when it is evident that no other
means could be pursued so effectual for its pre-
vention? The Duke of Bedford, as you observe
very properly, has a large stake in the country,
and he has had the sense to discern the only proper
means of preserving it; he is a REAL ALARMIST,
an alarmist upon rational motives. Mr. Pitt and
you, Sir, have no stake in the country, and rash
measures are well adapted to men of desperate
fortunes.

I shall

I shall therefore attempt a syllogism in a different mode, and your judges and mine, the public, shall determine who is in the right.

The French Revolution originated in the lavish Expenditure of the public money:

But the Duke of Bedford and the Earl of Lauderdale have endeavoured to restrain the lavish Expenditure of Administration:

Ergo, they took the only rational means of preventing in this country a calamity similiar to what has taken place in France.

Thus, Sir, I think your argument completely turns upon yourself. Because the two noble persons in question have called for an enquiry concerning your pension, you endeavour to infinuate against them a charge of desiring to produce a Revolution similar to that in France. If they had not objected to your pension, you would never have thought of such a charge. Now, as it happens, they have been acting in direct opposition to those principles and that line of conduct, which you would darkly, insidiously, and dishonestly charge them with; the real Revolutionary Committee, if there be one, consists of Edmund Burke, of William Pitt, of James (commonly called) Lord Grenville, and others their wicked abettors, who have wantonly

G   plunged

plunged the nation in a feries of rafh, precipitate, profufe, and ruinous meafures; who have neither the fkill and ability fuccefsfully to conduct a war, nor to negociate a peace.

If every man in England, Sir, who thinks 4000l. per annum from the public purfe, in times of fcarcity and wretchednefs, a reward above your deferts and your neceffities, is to be confidered as a Jacobin, then indeed is there caufe for alarm, the club is indeed formidably numerous, fince every man with whom I have converfed, of every party, is agreed in the fentiment. Nay, I will venture to affert, that the minifter himfelf, muft in this refpect be a Jacobin in his heart. Profufe and improvident as he is, and though he fpare no expence to gratify a favourite whim, to atchieve any felfifh purpofe, he muft not only think, but he muft know that this is a moft fcandalous perverfion of his power, a moft inexcufable profufion of the public treafure.

You are particularly unfortunate in your allufions to the French Revolution. By your former abfurd pamphlet on this fubject, you provoked the anfwer of Thomas Paine, and whatever mifchief his publication has done, is ultimately to be referred to you. By your comparifons between the

ftate

ſtate of the two countries, you excited a diſcuſſion, which left few men unintereſted in the diſpute. You infuſed jealouſies, ſuſpicions, and alarms, into one party; you called up the indignation of the other, by your ſpirit of intolerance and perſecution. Now, in truth and reaſon, the Britiſh nation had not the remoteſt concern with the French Revolution—Their buſineſs was to have viewed the ſtorm as ſpectators, from their happy eminence of national proſperity. If the firſt attempts of the Conſtituent Aſſembly had ſucceeded; if a good, ſtable, and permanent government could have been inſtituted, with a ſmaller portion of influence than we have given to our executive government, I grant that it would have afforded a precedent in this country, for ſome gentle and moderate reforms, which it would have been the intereſt of government to propoſe themſelves. The attempt did not ſucceed, becauſe, I agree with you, the French carried their projects of reform to a viſionary extreme; but all this we might have regarded as calm ſpectators, we *muſt* have regarded as ſuch, while the majority of this nation was in the full enjoyment of peace and proſperity.

The very ſmall party in this kingdom, which after the tenth of Auguſt remained attached to French principles (and that it was a ſmall party,

the

the affociations in 1792 fufficiently demonftrated)
were foon difgufted with the fucceeding atrocities.
At this moment, though many circumftances have
occurred, chiefly the work of you and your party,
to prevent unanimity on this queftion, I folemnly
declare, that I do not know a man, I have never
converfed with a man, who approves of *all* that
has been done in France. Some things all muft
approve in the French Revolution, fome things
you have approved yourfelf; for you have not yet
been hardy enough to deny the neceffity of a
reform in that government. Of many things,
men of fenfe will hefitate before they decide—Of
many, all good men muft entertain a juft abhor-
rence. Some of the atrocities, which have been
committed in France, appear to have been the
refult of that peculiarly difficult and unfortunate
fituation in which that nation was placed; a fituation that naturally difpofes to fufpicion, jealoufy,
and party rancour and malignity; powerfully affail-
ed from without, and confpired againft within; or,
as emphatically defcribed by a writer, whofe religion and charity I wifh you could imitate —
" Without were fightings, within were fears"—
Some of the crimes in which they have been involved, were the inevitable confequences of that
deep-rooted fyftem of corruption, which an un-
wife and profligate government had foolifhly che-
rifhed,

rifhed; as neceffary to its exiftence—Some were
the effects of perverfe paffions, of fpecious vil-
lainy, and of that philofophy, " falfely fo called,"
which I agree with you in reprobating, which
releafes men from the fear of God.—

Of all this we might have been inactive, though
melancholy fpectators ; and the more flagitious the
conduct of the French, the lefs dangerous would
have been their example.   But fome men are vul-
garly, though expreffively characterized, as de-
lighting " to fifh in troubled waters," and I know
no man to whom this character more applies than
yourfelf.

The fucceeding pages of your pamphlet, it
would be an outrage on humanity to criticife with
feverity.   The wanderings of a difturbed imagination command our pity.

A large portion of your pamphlet is, indeed,
only fit to be bound up with Quarle's Emblems,
Bunyan's Holy War, and other high efforts of
genius in the regions of myfticifm and allegory.
Your fneer on geometricians and chemifts, only
ferves to difplay your poverty and your pride; to
inform the public in a handfome manner, that you
underftand neither of thefe fciences.   The pun on

fergeants

sergeants at law is contemptible; and this is suc-
ceeded by a feries of jokes upon convents and
priors, beneath the conviviality of a porter-houfe.
But for thefe I refign you to the rebuke of your
confeffor, who will doubtlefs enjoin a proper penance
for having treated in a ludicrous manner, matters
of fo *facred* a nature as the *revenues* of the
church.

Your compaffion for " the print of the poor ox
that we fee in the fhop windows at Charing-crofs,"
is in the fame ftyle; it is ridiculous even beyond
your happieft efforts, when you mean to be moft
ferious; and your tranfition to Lord Keppel's pic-
ture, from that of the ox, is really as if you had
intended it as a burlefque upon your deceafed
friend, whofe eulogium you conclude, by affuring
your readers, that " he was no great clerk."
You may apologife for all this as the " garrulity of
age;" for my own part, I fee no purpofe in it,
unlefs you meant to involve a plain queftion in
ftudied obfcurity.

On one topic, however, I will undertake to fet
your heart at eafe. You feem more than ordina-
rily folicitous, left you fhould be fuppofed to coun-
tenance " a peace with regicides."—Truft me, Sir,
no man, who is acquainted with your habits, principles,

ciples, and temper, will ever fufpect you of the
ambition of appearing in the character of a *peace-
maker*—" A peace with regicides"—I can join you
as heartily and fincerely as any man, in deploring
the fate of the unfortunate monarch, to whom you
allude—But is no compaffion due to the fate of the
thoufands and *tens* of *thoufands*, that have fallen in
this difaftrous conteft ? Men of like *parts* and
paffions with the monarch whom you lament—and
can the human intellect be fo difordered, as to
mourn with deep-felt anguifh the death of a *fingle
man*, and to be callous to that complicated mifery,
which war entails on fo large a portion of the
human race ?

You have fhewn yourfelf fufficiently fenfible to
the affliction, with which you have been vifited
within the circle of your own family; I have faid,
and I repeat it, that I fincerely fympathife in
your forrow ; but I confefs that my aftonifhment is
excited beyond the powers of expreffion, at the
little of moral or religious inftruction, which fo
diftreffing and melancholy an event appears to have
imparted to your mind. You, Mr. Burke, have
been a parent ; you are inconfolable for the lofs of
a beloved and promifing child—Reflect, then, I
befeech you, for a moment, how many tender and
affectionate parents are made childlefs by this

3   wanton

wanton, this deteftable profufion of blood; for
which you are not afhamed to appear as an advo-
cate—" Thy fword hath made women childlefs,
fo fhall thy mother be childlefs among women,"
was the reproof of a prophet to a tyrant and war-
rior of antiquity.—Reflect, Sir, I intreat you, how
many excellent and valuable lives, the flower of
England, of Germany, and of France, are daily
cut off in this execrable conteft, not by the ftroke
of providence, but by the malice and depravity of
man.—" Me have ye bereaved of my children,
and brought down my grey hairs with forrow to
the grave," is the involuntary exclamation that
will iffue from the bleeding heart of many a
wretched parent, and will be recorded in judgment
againft the wicked abettors of this moft wicked
war.

I do not afk you, Sir, are you a Chriftian?---
The unbounded charity which that holy religion
prefcribes will not extend fo far, as to admit of the
proftitution of the term by applying it to any man,
who can entertain fuch principles. No fophiftry
of the church of Rome, no pretendedly facred
authority or delegation from Heaven, no abfolu-
tion from councils or from Popes can reconcile the
maffacre of mankind with the religion of Chrift---
No foothing unction on a death-bed can admi-
nifter

nifter peace to that foul that has trifled in this manner with every precept of its God.

Your heroes of chivalry had indeed fomething to plead in their excufe ; they might have devoted to death their feilow creatures on fome miftaken principles of honour; yet they fubjeĉted *them* to no dangers of which they did not partake; their vaffals fuffered no evils which they did not fhare themfelves. Their campaigns were not made in the clofet, but in the field. But if there is a cha-raĉter to be detefted above every other, it is that malignant, cowardly difpofition, which promotes quarrels, though it fears to meet them; which bufies itfelf only in exciting the bad paffions of mankind; feduces an ignorant and thoughtlefs multitude to murder one another; and while it provokes to mifchief, fhrinks from the confliĉt, fkulks like a recreant behind the baggage, views from a diftance the evil it has created; and feafts with a favage joy on human mifery, while it re-pofes itfelf in the moft perfeĉt fecurity. A cha-raĉter fimilar to this is only to be found in an an-cient book, with which I wifh you were better ac-quainted ; but which, in obedience to the canons of a certain church, you perhaps have refrained from perufing---The character to whom I allude, was " a liar and a murderer from the beginning;" and

H   being

being eternally wretched himfelf, he finds his only
folace in the act of inflicting mifery on others. If
you have any confcience, any feeling, any pre-
tence to religion, you will burn the pamphlet you
have announced; and for what you have already
done, you will repent in fackcloth and afhes.

To fay that I expect this act of virtue from you,
would be affectation. You will publifh, I dare
fay, and you will attempt to fupport the odious argument on fome fophiftical plea of expediency or
ftate neceffity---I fhall therefore referve myfelf for
the confideration of this part of the fubject till your
threatened pamphlet makes its appearance. But
in the mean time, I will warn you of what the
public will expect in that pamphlet. They will expect you to explain, in precife and definite terms,
what never has been yet explained---The real motives of miniftry in provoking this moft difaftrous,
this ill-omened war. They will expect you to
prove, in intelligible language, the *right* which
they affumed to interfere in the internal government of an indepedant ftate. You muft demonftrate what *profit* and emolument we were to derive from a conteft, which was likely to coft more
blood than a whole continent could redeem, and
more treafure than would purchafe both the Indies
---What folid reafons there were to depart from a
neutrality

neutrality truly enviable---To relinquiſh the unpre-
cedented advantage of a monopoly of the whole
commerce of the world. We ſhall look for ſome
explanation of the myſterious conference at Pilnitz;
of the compact on which the famous circular of
Pavia was founded.

We ſhall not admit, Sir, of thoſe circular arguments, thoſe crocodile ſyllogiſms, by which the
abſurd meaſures of adminiſtration have been
hitherto defended. Believe me, Sir, the nation is
no longer in a temper to be miſled by metaphors,
to be duped by declamation. The people will no
longer bear to be told " that miniſters engaged in
war in order to prevent war."—That " a ſtate of
hoſtility is eſſential to the preſervation of peace."—
That " plots exiſted which could no where be
found; and conſpiracies without conſpirators."—
That " inſurrection and riot are prevented by public calamity; and that rebellion is the neceſſary
conſequence of general content and proſperity."
Theſe, and other equally wiſe and juſt maxims,
with which you and our ſapient miniſters have ſo
often amuſed yourſelves, and deluded others, will
not now be endured. The people's blood muſt
not be ſhed for the ſake of an antitheſis; nor
the public treaſure ſquandered in ſupport of a
paradox.

The

The people will reprobate the blafphemous affertion, " That we have been fighting for God and Religion !"—They will ridicule the affumption, that " we are to fight for peace." No, Sir, the people now demand folid arguments, open proof, pofitive and overbearing reafons. The fervour of enthufiafm is now cooled; it is quenched with blood. The terrors which have been raifed by childifh and improbable fictions are now abated. " What advantage can we poffibly gain by perfevering in the conteft ?" is the univerfal exclamation ; and thefe advantages they will expect you to demonftrate upon the evident and infallible principles of vulgar arithmetic, and not on your metaphyfical proportions, your moral mathematics, which is in truth no other than the art of fubftituting words in the place of ideas.

I have the honour to be, Sir,

, Your's, &c.

Weftpark, March 5, 1796.

R. P.